For Tom

First published 1988 by Walker Books Ltd
87 Vauxhall Walk, London SE11 5HJ

© 1988 Inga Moore

First printed 1988
Printed in Hong Kong by
South China Printing Co.

British Library Cataloguing in Publication Data
Moore, Inga
Fifty red night-caps.
I. Title
823 [J]   PZ7

ISBN 0-7445-0794-4

FIFTY RED NIGHT- CAPS

Inga Moore

WALKER BOOKS

LONDON

Nico lived with his nan, in
a little wooden house in the hills.

One day Nico's nan brought home
a basket of red wool. She knitted fifty red
night-caps.

She asked Nico to take them to market.
"Mind you get a good price," she called
after him, as he set off carrying the
night-caps in a big bag.

Now, that bag was heavy and Nico hadn't
gone far before he felt hot and tired. So in
the cool shade of the forest he stopped
to rest. He put on a night-cap and curled up
under the trees.

He hadn't noticed the monkeys in the
branches overhead. As he slept, they swung
silently down to the ground.

They tiptoed over to Nico's bag.
They pulled out the night-caps and put
them on, one after another, until the
bag was empty.

Then back into the trees they
scampered, with such a din of excited
shrieks and chatter that Nico woke up.

He saw forty-nine monkeys wearing
forty-nine night-caps!

Poor Nico! How was
he going to get the night-caps back?
It was useless trying to catch the monkeys;
the higher he climbed . . .

the higher *they* climbed.

Perhaps he could lure them down
with some fruit.

But the monkeys had plenty of fruit
of their own.

Nico was beginning to
think he would *never* get the
night-caps back. He thought of all
the hours his nan had spent knitting them.
   He threw the fruit away. He hurled it
into the trees. It hit a monkey on the nose!

The monkeys threw their fruit back
at Nico, hitting him hard.

"Ow!" yelled Nico, losing his temper.
"Ow! You horrible, horrible monkeys!"
In his rage, he pulled off his night-cap and
flung it on the ground.

The monkeys shrieked.
Then *they* pulled off *their* night-caps
and flung them on the ground.

Quickly Nico gathered them up
and put them back into the bag.

Then off he went on his way to market.

He sold all fifty red night-caps for a good price.
He bought a new shirt, some slippers for his nan
and a fat, silver fish for dinner.

What a day it had been for Nico.
But he had helped his nan after all –
and he had certainly learned something
about monkeys.

Have you guessed what it was?